THE MAKING OF A NINJA!

Adapted by **Nicole Johnson**

Based on the screenplay by **Seth Rogen & Evan Goldberg & Jeff Rowe**,
and **Dan Hernandez & Benji Samit**

Illustrated by **Patrick Spaziante**

A Random House PICTUREBACK® Book

Random House 🏠 New York

rhcbooks.com
ISBN 978-0-593-64687-8 (trade)—ISBN 978-0-593-70758-6 (proprietary)
Printed in the United States of America
10 9 8 7 6 5 4 3 2

Leonardo, Raphael, Michelangelo, and Donatello may have been born regular turtles, but they were also born to be heroes! The crime-fighting brothers were just hatchlings when a mysterious ooze leaked down into their sewer home, transforming them into mutants! But as the brothers learned, you need more than just mutant powers to be a heroic ninja!

The first thing every ninja needs is a team, where each member brings their own special talents to the group. The leader of the Teenage Mutant Ninja Turtles is Leonardo. His confidence and hard work guide the Turtles in the right direction. And he's always ready to hype up his brothers before they face a tough challenge!

Raphael is the toughest Turtle around! With no fear and a lot of strength, Raph will run headfirst into any fight and probably win it. He's loyal to his brothers and loves being a part of their Turtle team, but he's also excited to make friends outside the sewers.

Michelangelo makes it his job to keep his team laughing . . . or at least he tries to! The friendliest of the Turtles, Mikey loves improv comedy and would rather resolve a conflict with a joke than a fight. He always has a positive attitude and wants to keep team spirits up!

MIKEY

Donatello is the brains behind the other Turtles' brawn. With his bo staff, he can hold up in a fight just as well as his brothers. Thanks to his smarts and great fighting skills, Donnie can sometimes seem a little arrogant, but that's just because he knows there's so much he has to offer the world!

Every ninja needs a good teacher. Luckily, these ninjas in training have Splinter, their sensei and father figure. He took the Turtles in when they were young and taught them ninjutsu so they could protect themselves.

He also taught the Turtles that ninjas need some great gear! In addition to Donnie's bo staff, Mikey has nunchucks, Raph can really make a point with his sai, and Leo always keeps his katanas close.

As the Turtles got older, they wondered if all there was to life was sewers and pizza. After all, a ninja needs a purpose! It was when they were out getting a pizza that they discovered theirs.

The brothers saw someone stealing a scooter and followed the thief to get it back. That's when they found out that fighting crime and helping people was what they were meant to do with their incredible skills.

The bike belonged to the one and only April O'Neil. And it's a good thing they met her, because a ninja needs trusted friends to help them on their missions.

April writes for her school paper and told the Turtles about some seedy stuff she discovered going on in the city by someone called Superfly. The Turtles knew that they couldn't just sit around and do nothing. This was what they'd been waiting for! Maybe if they could capture a bad guy, the city would celebrate them as heroes, and they could do things other teenagers do.

The Turtle team took their training from the sewers to the streets! For months they took down baddies all over the city and followed leads to find out where Superfly could be. Because a ninja isn't just cool looks and awesome gear. A ninja needs training, practice, and persistence to achieve their goals!

Soon they felt strong enough to take on the mystery April had been investigating.

Another important part of being a ninja is knowing who your enemy is. That's why the Turtles snuck up on a super-secret meeting between Superfly and his team. And good thing they did, because the Turtles found out that Superfly and his crew were mutants just like them!

The brothers had never met other mutants, and at first, they didn't want to fight them. But once they figured out Superfly's evil plan, the Turtles knew that the right thing to do was to stop Superfly and his team before they hurt anyone.

The most important part of being a ninja is having a heroic spirit! Even when things got hard, the Turtles never gave up, which inspired the other mutants to be heroes, too.

At first, the Turtles and Superfly's team fought against each other. But eventually, the other mutants realized that the Turtles were right to protect the city from Superfly's plan. They decided to work with the Turtles instead. Together, the mutants stopped Superfly and saved the city!

So there you have it: how to be a ninja! Sometimes it's about cool gear and fighting bad guys. But mostly, it's about being who you are and finding a way to make the world a better place.

Cowabunga!